Pachanga
Dance party

Los Jazz Bugs
The Jazz Bugs

La banda de las termitas
The termite band

Con cariño
With affection

¡Buena suerte!
Good luck!

La selva
The jungle

Norte
North

Sur
South

Tú estás aquí.
You are here.

¿Qué te pasa?
What's with you?

¡Ay, caramba!
Oh, my gosh!

¿Cómo llego a la…?
How do I get to the…?

¿Qué te pasa?
What's up?

¿Cómo estás?
How are you?

"¡Vamos ya!"
Let's go already!

Pa'arriba y pa'abajo
High and low

El Termite Nook
The Termite Nook

Pachanga esta noche
Party tonight

Hola
Hi

Mis amigos
My friends

Enemigos
Enemies

Señor Mosca
Mr. Fly

Americana
American

Señoras y señores
Ladies and gentlemen

¿Qué te pasa, calabaza?
What's up, pumpkin?

Es nuestra pachanga.
It's our party.

Uno, dos, tres
One, two, three

No seas loco.
Don't act crazy.

Cuatro, cinco, seis
Four, five, six

Aléjate un poco.
Move away from here.

Mi ritmo es caliente.
My rhythm's hot.

No te comas a mi gente.
Don't eat up my people.

Español
Spanish

¡Adiós!
Good-bye!

Es bueno
It's good

Cerrado
Closed

¡Hasta luego!
See you later!

Cuídate mucho.
Take good care.

Se habla español.
Spanish spoken here.

Clave
Clave rhythm

JAZZ FLY 2
The Jungle Pachanga

Wherein
Los Jazz Bugs
Meet
*La banda
de las termitas*

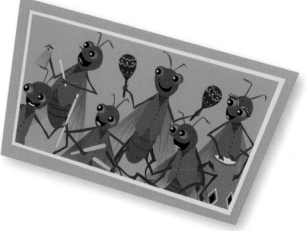

Written and performed by Matthew Gollub
Illustrated by Karen Hanke

 Tortuga Press Santa Rosa, California

Printed in China

Book Design by Karen Hanke
Musical Score written by Ylonda Nickell
Print Management by The Kids At Our House

Artwork in *Jazz Fly 2*: *The Jungle Pachanga* was rendered as traditional pencil sketches
which were scanned and recreated in Adobe Illustrator.
Gracias to Anakarina Sánchez who contributed additional vocals to the audio CD.

Library of Congress Cataloging-In-Publication Data

Gollub, Matthew.
    Jazz fly 2 : the jungle pachanga / written and performed by Matthew Gollub; illustrated by Karen Hanke.
    p. cm.
    SUMMARY: A fly uses a combination of Spanish and jazz scat to ask a sloth, a monkey,
    and a macaw to transport his band to a tropical concert site, and then to talk sense to
    an anteater who interrupts their performance. Includes author's note on how language,
    rhythm, color, and life are depicted in the book.
    ISBN 978-1-889910-44-4 (hardcover with audio cd : alk. paper)
    ISBN 978-1-889910-45-1 (pbk. with audio cd : alk. paper)

[1. Stories in rhyme. 2. Jazz–Fiction. 3. Musicians–Fiction.
4. Spanish language–Fiction. 5. Flies–Fiction.
6. Insects–Fiction. 7.Jungles–Fiction.]
I. Hanke, Karen, ill. II. Title. III. Title: Jazz fly
two. IV. Title: Jungle pachanga.

PZ8.3.G583Jbe 2010   [E]–dc22
2009024367
(HC) 10 9 8 7 6 5 4 3

To Jan Lieberman, lifelong librarian,
And to children everywhere who feel the rhythm of foreign words.
Con cariño. – M.G.

For Kris.
– K.H.

Special thanks to Tim Gennert, an audio production wizard with vision.
And to Ylonda Nickell, Queen of Alto Sax, for writing the musical score.

NOTE TO READER:
Jazz words in green,
Spanish words in fuchsia.
Good reading and good luck!
(¡Buena suerte!)

LA SELVA
(THE JUNGLE)

NORTE

SUR

TÚ ESTÁS AQUÍ
(YOU ARE HERE)

Zippidy-BING!

A tropical tour.
The fly drove his band, nicely dressed,
on their way to playin' music
in a termite nest.

But the limousine sputtered, the gas ran dry, so the fly popped the hood and started clangin' with a wrench:

Conk! Conk! Conk! Conk-conk!

"*¿Qué te pasa?*"
said a sloth
with a puzzled look.

The band had to reach the Termite Nook,
so the fly started flippin' through his Spanish phrase book.
He said:
"CHOO-ka CHOO-ka TING.
*¡Ay, caramba! ¿Cómo cómo llego
a la* CHOO-ka *pachanga?*"

Jazz-Spanish

The sloth
let the band
climb on its back
but seven seconds later,
stopped for a nap.

ZZZZZZ...

A screechin'
spider monkey darted
through the trees
and heard the fly's cry
on the tropical breeze:

"CHOO-ka CHOO-ka TING.
¡Ay, caramba!
¿Cómo cómo llego
a la CHOO-ka pachanga?"

"*¿Qué te pasa?*" said the monkey,
"*¿Cómo cómo estás?*"
The monkey let the
Jazz Bugs cling to its side,
then gave the band
a stomach-churning,
acrobatic ride.

The Jazz Bugs landed with antennas twisted.
One last time, the fly persisted:

"CHOO-ka CHOO-ka TING. ¡Ay, caramba!
¿Cómo cómo llego
a la CHOO-ka pachanga?"

"*¡Vamos ya!*" a painted bird
began to caw, so the band caught
a ride with an orange macaw.

Pa'arriba y pa'abajo. High and low,
they zoomed through the canopy, then let go....

Down they
parachuted
through the
termite nest,
where the
glowworm waiters
served the
very best
rotten twigs
to termites and
nectar to grubs.

EL
TERMITE
NOOK
PACHANGA ESTA NOCHE
(PARTY TONIGHT)

SALIDA

"LOS JAZZ BUGS"

The house band scurried off
the lit stage as the managing moth
fluttered down from his loft:

"¡Hola, welcome, mis amigos!
I thought you had been eaten
by our enemigos."

"ZAH!" the fly counted,
"HA-ba-da DOON, ZEE-ZAY!"
Willie the Worm twanged the bass:
Buh-DIH-buh-dih DOO-DOON...
Centipede Sam joined the jam:
DA-dee, GA-gee...

"LOS
JAZZ
BUGS"

Then out strode Nancy
in her red rose gown
with her sax, mascara, and
her big gnat sound:

Dwee-DAY, Dwee-DAY,
Dwee-dee-DAY...
Dwee-DAY, Dwee-DAY,
Dwee-dee-DAY.

A ladybug caught the Jazz Fly's eye,
made his drumsticks bounce
—Skiddily BOP—oh my!

"*Señor Mosca.*
My name is Juana.
Your music's
so...*americana.*"

The Jazz Fly's chest nearly
leapt from his vest.
He sailed up through the nest and
burst the night into bop:

HA-buh-duh DOOM,
ZEE-buh-duh-BOING,
ZOP-BRRRING Baby!
BOOM! Skiddily BOP,
Za-ba ZEE, Za-BAM!

Insects swarmed
to dig the rippin' sound
till the fly caught
the ear of somethin'
big on the ground.
The nest
started
shakin'....
The termites
were
quakin'....

"LOS JAZZ BUGS"

A claw slashed
a hole…
in the wall
that was gapin'!

A whip-like tongue shot straight to the stage,
slurpin' chairs, tables, bug pomade
and the managing moth's pink lemonade!

"LOS JAZZ BUGS"

"*Señoras y señores,* we are under attack.
Our only hope now is to divide and distract.
Take care of your young. Hold your pupa tight,
and please come again on some other night."

the conga...

The termite house band
grabbed the tools of their trade
to confuse the anteater
with the beats they played on

maracas...

the bongo...

and bell...

the claves...

and timbales...

which the termites
played like...CRAZY!

The Jazz Fly buzzed outside of the nest and hovered before the anteater's eyes. Again, he flipped through his Spanish phrase book for the words he still didn't know. Then…he…

...loosened his tie.
He wriggled his feet.
He bobbed his head with
a Latin beat, and said:

CHOO-ka CHOO-ka TING. *¡Ay, caramba!*
¿Qué te pasa, calabaza?
Es nuestra pachanga.
Uno, dos, tres. No seas loco.
Cuatro, cinco, seis. ¡Aléjate un poco!
TAKA-TON TING.
Mi ritmo es caliente.
RRAKA-DON-ga DON.
*¡No te comas a mi gente!**

* Which means, roughly translated,
HABA DOO-BA DING. Make a move from here.
Come on, pumpkin. Can't you hear?
1,2,3. My rhythm's HOT....4,5,6, eat my people NOT!

The fly's Latin rhythm and his *español*
attracted a huge spotted cat on patrol.
What a chilling surprise to see
the jade green eyes

as the jaguar pounced,
stretched to full size!
The jaguar chased
the beast from the nest
as the fly bid
the anteater,
"¡Adiós!"

On till dawn, the two bands played. Larvae danced.
A thousand eggs were laid. The rain forest chattered. Word got 'round 'bout
the Spanish-speakin' fly who really brought the house down.

"*Es bueno*," said the moth,
"that you learned *español*.
Another language helps when
you're in a hole.

CERRADO
(CLOSED FOR
REPAIR).

"The sloth and the
monkey say they found
your next gig.
From now on you'll
be playin'...

Uno, dos. ¡Uno, dos, tres, cuatro!

LOVE ♥ JAZZ

S.S. SPANISH SPOKEN

S.S. Se

...on an ocean rig." And here's what it sounded like when the Jazz Bugs

Rrraka-taka, Don!　¡Hasta luego!

Cuídate mucho.

HABLA ESPAÑOL

left the jungle and set sail on the Caribbean Sea.

Author's Note

Language, rhythm, color, life!

These four themes shone like flashlights in the jungle and revealed details that led to this musical book.

Language I grew up speaking English and began Spanish in 7th grade. Later, I traveled to Spanish-speaking countries where friends, children, and almost everyone I met helped me learn new phrases and words. The wit and warmth of Spanish speakers encouraged me, and I continue to benefit from speaking Spanish to this day. A third language this book features is "jazz" or "scat": rhythmic, nonsensical words that don't appear in the dictionary. In the spirit of African-American jazz masters, I created words like CHOO-ka TING, and ZEE-buh-duh BOING. To create your own scat phrases, combine interesting consonants and vowels. Then try saying the words with lots of expression.

Rhythm My narration starts out in a rhythm called "swing." The swing changes to "Latin" whenever someone speaks Spanish. Swing has a lilting feel set to three notes per beat (triplets), which complements the cadence of spoken English. Latin rhythms, which are set to four notes per beat, sound a little busier than swing. Spanish likewise sounds busier than English, since virtually every vowel in Spanish gets its own syllable. The unifying beat in Latin jazz is the *clave* (KLAH-veh), played, logically enough, on the *claves*. Here's how the *clave* beat (in black notes) fits the "chorus."

CHOO-ka CHOO-ka ting.   ¡Ay,   Ca- ram- ba!

¿Cómo   cómo   llego a la   CHOO-ka Pa- chan- ga?

Color From camouflaged insects to the jaguar's coat, the rain forest presents a rich palette of colors. But "color" can also mean personal traits. Storytellers and illustrators enjoy giving their characters color, like the ladybug's foreign accent or the moth's special hairdo. Everyone has color when you stop to think about it. Just look for the characteristics that make each person unique.

Life! In the jungle, intense sunlight, year-round warmth and plenty of rain make things grow fast. Insects multiply. Plants grow intertwined. To survive, plants and animals interact and adapt. Given these conditions, it wasn't hard to imagine how a ladybug might befriend a fly, how Spanish and jazz words could mix, or even how jungle critters could start using their own cell phones!

Language, rhythm, color, life! For you, these four themes may lead to something else: a painting, dance, photograph, maybe a song. Watch for the details in the jungle of your thoughts. Quietly. Patiently. There, what was that? Like termites, your unique ideas may be teeming below the surface.

—M. G.

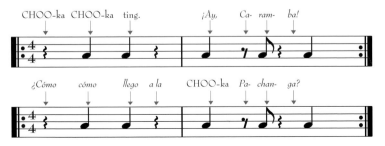

Pachanga
Dance party

Los Jazz Bugs
The Jazz Bugs

La banda de las termitas
The termite band

Con cariño
With affection

¡Buena suerte!
Good luck!

La selva
The jungle

Norte
North

Sur
South

Tú estás aquí.
You are here.

¿Qué te pasa?
What's with you?

¡Ay, caramba!
Oh, my gosh!

¿Cómo llego a la…?
How do I get to the…?

¿Qué te pasa?
What's up?

¿Cómo estás?
How are you?

"¡Vamos ya!"
Let's go already!

Pa'arriba y pa'abajo
High and low

El Termite Nook
The Termite Nook

Pachanga esta noche
Party tonight

Hola
Hi

Mis amigos
My friends

Enemigos
Enemies

Señor Mosca
Mr. Fly

Americana
American

Señoras y señores
Ladies and gentlemen

¿Qué te pasa, calabaza?
What's up, pumpkin?

Es nuestra pachanga.
It's our party.

Uno, dos, tres
One, two, three

No seas loco.
Don't act crazy.

Cuatro, cinco, seis
Four, five, six

Aléjate un poco.
Move away from here.

Mi ritmo es caliente.
My rhythm's hot.

No te comas a mi gente.
Don't eat up my people.

Español
Spanish

¡Adiós!
Good-bye!

Es bueno
It's good

Cerrado
Closed

¡Hasta luego!
See you later!

Cuídate mucho.
Take good care.

Se habla español.
Spanish spoken here.

Clave
Clave rhythm